Trey,
the Chef

Copyright © 2019 Kira Parris-Moore
All rights reserved
First Edition

NEWMAN SPRINGS PUBLISHING
320 Broad Street
Red Bank, NJ 07701

First originally published by Newman Springs Publishing 2019

ISBN 978-1-64096-763-2 (Hardcover)
ISBN 978-1-64096-764-9 (Digital)

Printed in the United States of America

Trey, the Chef

Kira Parris-Moore

Illustrated by Federica Fabbian

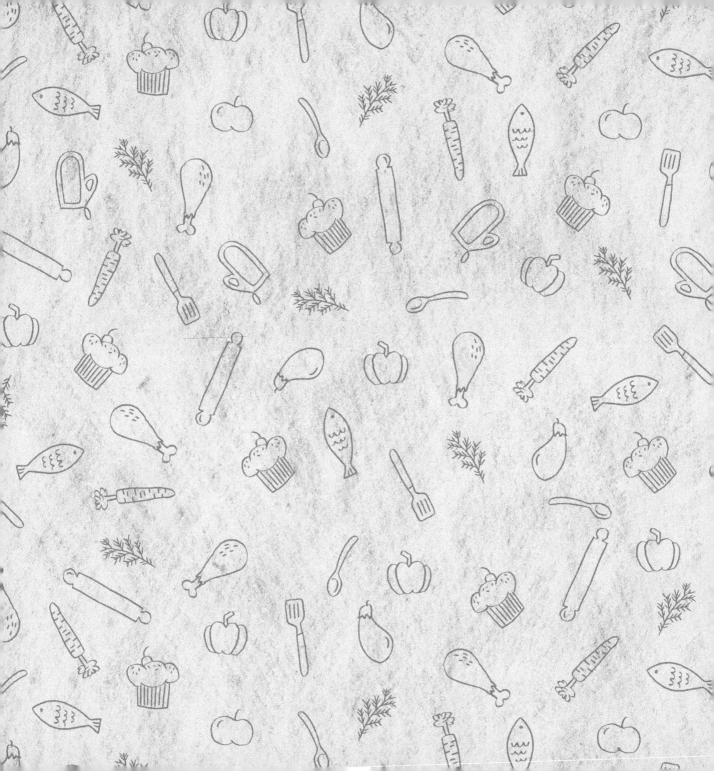

To my smart and very capable son, who I know will defy stereotypes to make his mark on the world. I have become a better person by being your mother.

I have a son.
His name is Trey.
He loves to create
marvelous dishes
all through
the day.

He bakes and shakes, spices and dices.
He loves to cook food in all different sizes.

His attention to detail is second to none.
He can make food delicious and plenty of fun.

There is one problem,
I must reveal.
When people call
his name in the kitchen,
he does not yield.
He does not speak
or follow directions.
He cannot give others
cooking lessons.

Trey has

AUT

Please don't feel sorry
or worry or fear.
His autism makes him a great chef
and well revered.

His dishes are delicious and packed
with plenty of taste.
He makes them with care,
no hurry or haste.

His autism is a gift,
a blessing from God.
Otherwise, I don't think
he would be so good at his job.

MY son
TREY

How to Cook Like Chef Trey

Salmon Croquettes

1. Empty two cans of salmon into a large bowl.
2. Take out any small bones from salmon.
3. Crack an egg into a bowl.
4. Mix the egg with the salmon.
5. Add diced onions and peppers to your liking.
6. Take a chunk of salmon mixture into your hands and mold them into patties.
7. Season salmon patties with salt and pepper.
8. Pour a generous amount of oil into a frying pan over medium heat.
9. Place patties into pan and cook patties until golden brown.

Elephant Ears

1. Sprinkle flour onto cutting board.
2. Take out canned biscuit dough and seperate pieces of dough.
3. Roll out dough until flat.
4. Fill up a pan halfway with oil over medium heat.
5. When hot, place in a few pieces of dough one at a time and fry until golden brown.
6. Flip dough to other side and fry until golden brown.
7. Take out pieces and place on a paper towel to drain oil.
8. Sprinkle with favorite toppings (powdered sugar, cinnamon sugar, whatever you like on your elephant ears!)

How to BE around someone with autism:

- BE kind to those with autism. Their brain is different, so they might make loud noises, rock themselves, or flap their hands. Remember even if they act strange or different, they are people too.

- BE patient to those with autism. Teach them everything you know but break it down into small steps. You might have to repeat these steps over and over again, but this helps them learn better.

- BE creative when dealing with someone who has autism. You can't treat people with autism the same because they are individuals in their own unique way.

- BE persistent and never give up! You will be surprised how much a difference this will make in their lives and yours!

About the Author

Kira Parris-Moore is a licensed Marriage and Family Therapist residing in Durham, NC. She is a wife and mother of two young boys, ages 7 and 3. Her passion is mental health and helping children who have developmental and behavioral health challenges. She has worked in the mental health field for 15 years with children and adolescents. She hopes that with her knowledge of mental health and gift for writing, she can have a positive impact on families struggling with these challenges.

About the Illustrator

 Federica Fabbian is an Italian artist living in France.

Illustration is her biggest passion and she has always been better at communicating by drawing, rather than by writing. She always tries to do so without taking herself too seriously.

CPSIA information can be obtained
at www.ICGtesting.com
Printed in the USA
LVHW071252200320
650689LV00020B/98

9 781640 967632